For my Mother ~
who doesn't like staying in bed either!
M.C.

For Tony Downham
G.W.

First published in the United States 1996 by
Little Tiger Press,
12221 West Feerick Street, Wauwatosa, WI 53222-2117
Originally published in Great Britain 1996 by
Magi Publications, London
Text © 1996 Michael Coleman
Illustrations © 1996 Gwyneth Williamson
CIP Data is available.
Printed in Belgium
First American Edition
ISBN 1-888444-04-5
1 3 5 7 9 10 8 6 4 2

Ridiculous!

by

Michael Coleman

Pictures by

Gwyneth Williamson

"Ho hum," yawned Mr. Tortoise. "Winter is here."
"So it is," yawned Mrs. Tortoise. "Come on,
Shelley, time for bed."

"But I don't feel sleepy yet," said Shelley.

"*Ridiculous!*" cried Mr. Tortoise. "All tortoises go to sleep for the winter."
"Why?" asked Shelley.
"Because it's cold outside and there's no food."

"But I don't want to go to sleep," said Shelley.
"I want to see what winter is like!"
"Ridiculous!" cried Mr. and Mrs. Tortoise together.
"Whoever heard of a tortoise outside in winter?"

Soon
Mr. Tortoise
began to snore . . .

. . . and not long
after that Mrs. Tortoise
began to snore . . .

. . . and not long after *that*, Shelley left her warm
bed of leaves, and out she went through a hole in
the shed to see what winter was like.

Outside the shed, Shelley blinked.
There was snow and ice everywhere, even on the
duck pond and the hill. As she lumbered along,
a duck spotted her.

"A tortoise out in winter?" quacked the duck.
"Ridiculous!"
"No it isn't," said Shelley.
"Oh no? Then let's see you break through the
ice to get food like *I* can. Ha-quack-ha!"
"He's right," thought Shelley. "I can't do that.
I don't have a beak."

As Shelley began to walk up the hill,
she met a dog.

"A tortoise out in winter?" barked the dog.
"Ridiculous!"
"No it isn't," said Shelley, feeling a little cross.
"Oh no? Then let's see you keep warm by
running around like *I* can. Ha-woof-ha!"
"He's right," thought Shelley sadly. "I can't
do that either."

The dog ran off after a cat, but the cat climbed up a tree. She looked down at Shelley.

"A tortoise out in winter?" meowed the cat.
"Ridiculous!"
"No it isn't," said Shelley, even more crossly.
"Oh no? Then let's see you run into a nice warm
house as quickly as *I* can. Ha-meow-ha!"
"She's right," thought Shelley, shivering with cold.
"I can't run like a dog or a cat. I'm just too slow!"

The cat raced off into her house before the dog could catch her, and Shelley trudged toward the top of the hill, where she met a bird.

"A tortoise out in winter?" cheeped the bird.
"Ridiculous!"
"No it isn't," snapped Shelley.
"Oh no? Then let's see you fly home
and cuddle up with your family like *I* can.
Ha-cheep-ha!"
"Of course I can't fly," thought Shelley.
"I can't even hop!"

Shelley felt cold and miserable. She remembered her warm, cozy bed, and a tear trickled down her cheek. "They're *all* right," she thought. "A tortoise out in winter *is* ridiculous!"

She was so sad she didn't notice the big patch of ice ahead.

. . . and she slipped on it!
Shelley fell over backward and began to slide
down the hill.
Faster and faster she went . . .

. . . faster than
a *dog* could run . . .

. . . faster than
a *cat* . . .

. . . until suddenly she
hit a bump . . .

. . . and flew into the
air like a *bird*.

Wheeee!
With a thump Shelley landed on the
icy duck pond and slid toward the hole
in the shed . . .

. . . but it was all covered up with ice!
"Ha-quack-ha, what did I say?" cried the
duck as she slid by him. "Where's your
beak to break the ice with?"
"I don't have a beak," thought Shelley.
"But I *do* have . . .

. . . a shell!"
And tucking her head inside it,
she broke through the ice,
into the shed and home!

Hearing all the noise, Mrs. Tortoise woke up.
"You haven't been outside, have you, Shelley?"
she asked.

"A tortoise out in winter?" said Shelley,
snuggling into bed. And before she could say
"Ridiculous!"
she was fast asleep.